The Cramp Twins

created by brian wood

Bloomsbury

First published in Great Britain in 1995.
Text and illustration copyright © 1995.
Brian Wood.

The moral right of the author has been asserted.
Bloomsbury Publishing PLC, 2 Soho Square, London W1V 6HB.
A CIP catalogue record for this book is available from The British Library
ISBN 0 7475 2078 X
Printed in Singapore.

Lucien Cramp woke up **Screaming.**

He'd been having the most terrible **nightmare.**

The same nightmare he'd been having all week.

In his dream Lucien found himself walking through the streets, naked except for a giant nappy.

The whole town had turned out to watch and they were laughing. Laughing at him!

wrapping himself in his quilt,
Lucien shuffled over to the
window, just to make sure it had
all been a dream.

Outside, the streets of
Soap City were just as
quiet and dull as usual and

feeling better, he set off to the
bathroom to get cleaned up.

Lucien had a nose bleed and for
some reason his pyjamas
felt strangely moist.

Soap City was
deserted and the chimneys of the
Haz Chem soap factory were missing
their usual clouds of lemon~fresh steam. 🌼

Today was a town holiday and the good
folks of Soap City were busy getting
ready for the Haz Chem
Country and western
barbecue.

Almost everyone in Soap City
worked at the soap factory and everyone
at the factory was automatically a member
of the Country and western club.

No one could remember why it was
a Country·and western club but everyone got
to wear cool outfits so no one complained.

The Haz Chem barbecue was the top social event of the year in the town and all the kids looked forward to it just as much as Christmas.

All the kids that is, except Lucien.

For as long as Lucien could remember, the annual b a r b e c u e had been his family's 'number one', 'top' chance to embarrass him in front of the whole town.

At last year's barbecue, his twin brother wayne had secretly entered him for the 'Man Mountain' strong~man contest.

After six trials of strength, Lucien came last and was beaten by at least three girls, one of them still wearing a nappy. ▲▲▲

Lucien made up his mind to run away from home. But before he left, he decided to have one last bowl of his favourite Captain Power breakfast cereal. He would need all the energy he could get for the long walk to the bus stop.

From the kitchen window he could see his brother Wayne sitting on the front step trying to sell a dead dog to some little kids from down the road.

PUPPY
For sale:

Shuddering in disgust, he picked up the economy box of cereal only to find it was empty. Wayne must have eaten the whole lot for breakfast.

On any other day Lucien would have shouted for his mum to get another box,

but today he would be wasting his breath. The house was empty.

Dad was putting up tents for the barbecue and Mum was locked in the garden shed, finishing off the twins' top-secret cowboy outfits.

Lucien went to the back door and stared at the **No Entry** sign his mum had hung on the shed door.

The exact design of the twins' barbecue costumes was always kept top-secret but the theme of Cowboy Cleaners was the same every year.

↑ 'Mop Avenger'   ↖ 'Captain Bleach'

Last year, Lucien went as the 'Mop Avenger' and Wayne was 'Captain Bleach'.

Today Lucien didn't **care** what type of cowboy he was.

He had no doubt that this year's outfit would be just as hideous and embarrassing as the last, and the only thing stopping him running away that very second was the secret hope that wayne's costume might be more

horrible

than his.

Marshal meadow Fresh

←

Cheered up a little, Lucien went to his 'office' to send a good morning 'e~mail' message to his best friend Tony, only to discover that wayne had built a high~voltage electric fence around his desk.

A thoughtful note was attached;
'Danger! This will kill you!'
Lucien was worried. It was obvious that wayne wasn't in a good mood and worst of all his parents were out.

It's going to be a bad day,
Lucien thought to himself

and leaving nothing to chance, he
raced up to his room to finish off
the self~defence outfit he'd been
knitting for just such an occasion.
Lucien was good at knitting.

As it turned out, Lucien was
quite right. Wayne was in a bad mood.

He'd only managed to get 10p
and a packet of cheese and onion
crisps for his dead dog and worst
of all, his electric fence trap
was just as he'd left it.

Wayne couldn't bear to see all his hard work go to waste and he decided to electrocute himself instead.

Zizzzz.

Feeling energized, he set off to beat up his wimp brother. That always managed to cheer him up.

In his room, Lucien was warned of his brother's arrival by the smell of singed hair wafting up the stairs.

Keeping calm, he got into his self~defence outfit and waited...

wayne burst in the room like a wild thing and began battering Lucien with his hammer-like fists.

But Lucien's rubberized wool suit was more than a match for wayne's cruel blows and eventually wayne gave up, disappointed.

Moments later Lucien fainted. The stench of singed hair and dead spaniel was just too much.

Taking full advantage of his brother's unconsciousness, wayne began rummaging through Lucien's knitting bag in search of **weapons**.

Wayne emptied the whole bag, but found nothing of any use. Even Lucien's knitting needles were made of squishy plastic and he was about to give up the search, when he noticed something much more interesting.

Rubberized wool; **warning: shrinks when wet.**

Lucien came out of his doze to find Wayne grinning down at him.

Fearless inside his defensive shell, Lucien stood up, and made rude gestures to his brother.

Lucien braced himself for another violent attack, but to his surprise,

Wayne bundled him into the shower and turned on the tap.

Within seconds, the rubberized wool began to shrink and Lucien's eyes swelled up alarmingly.

Within a minute, Lucien was totally immobilized, trapped in a doll~size outfit. Wayne was pleased with his work, but didn't really know what to do with his new plaything.

In the end he bounced Lucien down to the living room and sat on the sofa with a kipper~and~peanut butter sandwich, content to watch his brother squirm around the room.

Lucien's suit was so tight, he couldn't call for help and he had to think up an alternative rescue plan...

After studying the situation for a while, Lucien had a bright idea and rolling across the room, he began to tap on the radiator with his foot ‡.

Wayne watched this extraordinary behaviour with great interest and as he did so, his eyes became all misty and a drop of saliva grew from his chin.

Wayne was thinking.

Next door, Lucien's best friend, Tony 'the shrimp boy' Parsons, was having lunch. At only twenty centimetres tall, Tony was the smallest ten-year-old in the world.

A baby fly

A baby Tony

The Parsons family were by far the strangest people in Soap City.

For one thing they had lived in their house long before the town was even built, when the whole place was still a swamp.

But the most bizarre thing about the Parsons was that everything they owned was brown, and in Soap City anything brown was uncool.

Tony's family were making a lot of noise eating their lunch and no one could hear Lucien's frantic tapping coming from the wall.

Mrs Parsons had made everyone bangers and mash but Tony was having his usual meal of extra-fine spaghetti.

Tony's mouth was just too small for anything else.

Although Mother Nature had condemned Tony to a never-ending diet of noodles, she had also been kind to him.

Like many small creatures, Tony had been blessed with super~keen senses and as soon as his family had stopped munching, his sub~sonic ears had no trouble tuning into the Morse code message coming from next door...

H.E.L.P.M.E.

G.E.T.M.U.M.

Biting off a spaghetti strand with his back teeth, Tony leapt from the table shouting,

Lucien needs me!

But the Parsons family didn't hear a thing. Tony's voice was just too quiet.

Back at the Cramp's house, Wayne's thoughtful slumber was interrupted by the sound of Tony coming through the cat~flap.

Tony was a blur.
Racing between Wayne's legs and under cushions, he surveyed the situation.

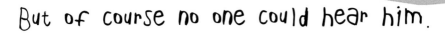

he shouted.

But of course no one could hear him.

Quick Sticks, Tony raced into the Cramp's back garden and under the shed door.

Tony froze.

The world had gone white and Tony wondered if he was dead.

Mrs Cramp was a little lady with a big idea. It all started when she looked at some cheese under a microscope at school.

A whole new world of dirt and decay was revealed to her and she was never the same again.

Cheesy Ming...

From that moment on, the young Mrs Cramp dedicated her life to the elimination of filth. She took no prisoners and had no mercy for grit, grime or grease.

Living in Soap City was a dream come true for Mrs Cramp.

But there was one thing not quite right in her whiter~than~white universe. Mr Cramp's overalls.

The very idea of cleaning those ground~in oil stains and stubborn odours was

enough to make her weep, and she longed for the day when her husband would get a nice office job with a nice clean suit.

But today all thoughts of **crusty** work~wear had been forgotten and Mrs Cramp was busy creating **the** most dazzling and memorable barbecue outfits ever.

According to town gossip, a new job had been created in the paper~clip department and Mrs Cramp was determined to get her husband noticed by all the 'big cheese' bosses down at the barbecue.

Judging by the expression on little Tony parsons' face, Mrs Cramp felt sure of success.

She put the cowboy outfit into
a bin~bag and the room
went dark...

Hello,
Tony dear.

Don't worry,
it won't
hurt you.

To be honest, she couldn't be absolutely
sure about that. The Sub~Atomic Whitener
she was using was never intended for
domestic use.

Oh...

was all that Tony
could manage.

Tony was in shock!

'Has Lucien sent you in here to **spy** on me?'

Mrs Cramp asked.

At that moment Tony remembered his friend in the front room and began to hop up and down, pointing to the house.

Mrs Cramp had known Tony Parsons all his life, and understood him perfectly.

Pausing only to padlock the shed door she grabbed Tony and marched back to the house.

A **scream** came from inside, closely followed by another...

Wayne was good at excuses and he filled the air with the best of them.

> Lucien is my best friend! He fell over! Tony did it! I would never hurt my brother! Please Mummy I feel sick!

But his mother wasn't paying him any attention. Her eyes were fixed on the floor.

w...w...woolly bits

she hissed, and with that she stomped out of the room...

The three boys looked at the floor. All they could see was a bit of fuzz stuck to the carpet.

Seconds later Mrs Cramp was back, this time driving her Mobivac ᵗᵐ six wheeler, industrial strength vacuum cleaner.

Almost instinctively the twins took cover.

Tony followed their lead and took refuge in what looked to him like a couple of cushions.

With just one skilful turn around the room Mrs Cramp had the offending fuzzy bit in the bag.

Feeling much relieved she drove
the Mobivac ™ back to the garage.
The room went quiet.

wayne was the first to emerge,
and feeling hungry after his
brush with **danger** he reached
down under the sofa for his lunch.

Not realizing that Tony parsons
was hiding in his sandwich...

wayne swallowed it down in one bite.

Lucien was in the hall waiting to be rescued when he heard his mum chasing Wayne around the living room.

BANG! Crash!

CRUNCH!

Judging by the struggle going on, Lucien guessed it must be bath time...

and sure enough, half an hour later both the boys were locked in the bathroom, waiting for the torture to begin.

paz pan

heavy-duty pan scrub.

Tony had **no** idea where he was. Looking at the amount of trash thrown around the place he felt sure he wasn't in the Cramp's living room any more. This room was dark and...

there was a strong smell of Captain Power breakfast cereal.

Feeling tired after all the excitement, he wandered off down a small round corridor and found a room with a bed in it.

Tony had a nap on Wayne's left kidney.

Mr Cramp had one dream in his life.
He wanted to be a **C o w b o y** .

For ten years he had worked like
a dog at the Country and western club
and for ten years the Executive Cowboy
Committee had passed him over for
promotion. Mr Cramp still held the
lowest rank of all: 'Farm-hand grade 3'.

But today his luck had changed.
Today Mr Cramp had spoken to the
biggest cowboy of them all. None
other than 'walter winkle', chairman
of the Haz Chem Corporation and
all-round biggest cheese in town.

Mr Winkle (who was Known as the 'Grand Bubba' when he was wearing his cowboy costume) had said;

'Get out of my way Norman!'

Which was almost right. Mr Cramp's middle name was Neville.

Mr Cramp was almost sick with joy after his chat with the Grand Bubba and he arrived home convinced that one of the ten-gallon cowboy hats in the trophy tent would be for him.

In fact he could think of only two things standing between him and his promotion and he was looking at both of them **right now**.

The twins had gone a funny red colour after their bath and from where Mr Cramp stood they looked just like a couple of little devils.

Devilish glow

Little devils sent to rob him of his lovely new cowboy hat, he thought to himself.

Leaving nothing to chance, Mr Cramp decided to use his ultimate weapon of last resort. The one threat he knew they would never ignore.

If you boys don't behave yourselves today I'll hand you over to your **mother** for her Beauty Experiments!

Lucien felt his tummy fill with ice-cold canal water. Mum's idea of beauty was too terrible to contemplate and he began to tremble.

Wayne, on the other hand, was wearing the same stupid grin he had worn all morning and Lucien was suspicious.

As it turned out Lucien was right to be suspicious. Wayne had been hatching a plot to embarrass his brother for weeks and his dad's new threat made his plan seem even better.

Wayne had secretly entered Lucien for the Hogs 'n' Hens square dance contest. His dance partner for the evening was to be none other than 'weepy wendy', the Grand Bubba's favourite daughter and the biggest cry~baby in town.

Wayne was sure that Lucien's shabby footwork would get wendy's tear factory working and he began to giggle to himself, imagining Lucien modelling one of Mum's experimental beauty products.

Fungus of the forest face~pack.

Wayne was still giggling when his mum came in the room dressed in her new cowboy outfit. Then the whole room exploded with laughter.

Ha! Ha! Ha! Ha!

Titter
Titter

Tony was woken up by the sound of laughter echoing all round him. His little heart leapt for joy. 'Rescue at last,' he thought and he began to **shout** for help.

But Tony's feeble little chirp was no use at all and in desperation he picked up a toy pram he'd found and began **smashing** it against the wall, hoping someone would hear him.

At that moment Wayne stopped laughing and fell over in a heap. His tummy was in uproar and he was about to start **whining** to his mum when she handed him a real reason to complain.

A brilliant white cowboy outfit, just like hers.

Lucien watched his brother's face collapse in horror and was about to let rip with his best belly~laugh when his mum handed him an outfit just the same.

The twins were **devastated**. This was the worst thing that could have happened. Not only did they have to wear stupid clothes but now everyone would know they were related.

There was an uncomfortable silence in the Cramp's car as it slid out of the drive and past the Parsons' house.

Chug Chug...

Lucien stared back at Tony's house and wondered what had happened to his friend. For as long as he could remember, Tony had gone to the barbecue in their car, and Lucien was worried.

Inside the Parsons' house, Tony's mum and dad still hadn't noticed their son was missing.

They mistakenly believed that an old coffee stain 🔹 in the front lounge was their son. Assuming he was studying for an important exam they had decided not to disturb him.

Meanwhile, someone had turned
the lights on in Wayne's tummy.

The sub~atomic whiteness of Wayne's
outfit was so powerful that his belly
was now bathed in a BRILLIANT glow
and Tony finally realized where he was.

Tony was overcome with emotion.

One moment he was jumping for joy,
and the next he was KICKING at
Wayne's innards, furious at Wayne
for eating him in the first place.

At least now he could plan his
escape and wasting no time, he
wandered off in search of an exit.

The Cramps were late for the barbecue
and as soon as they arrived Mrs Cramp
dragged the twins off to the women~only
'Hen House' where they were to be
exhibited in front of the executive mums.

For over half an hour the twins were
prodded and poked by a swarm of
over~perfumed executive ladies, all
eager to learn Mrs Cramp's secret
for whiter~than~white whites.

Mrs Cramp was more than happy to oblige
and the whole sorry affair would have
lasted all day if it hadn't been for
wayne's impromptu outburst...

Tony's wanderings had set off some unpleasant rumblings in wayne's tummy. Rumblings that wayne was unable to control...

Butt Quake !¡!

Bottom burps were the ultimate 'no~no' in such refined company and within a few seconds the tent was empty.

Seeing a chance to escape, the twins cut loose and ran off in opposite directions.

Lucien was having no fun at all without Tony and he allowed himself to drift along with the crowd, hoping to spot his friend scurrying around people's ankles.

Tony had a morbid fear of crowds and he had to wear a special hat with a flag pole on it just to avoid getting   squashed.

In all the years that Lucien and Tony had come to the barbecue, Lucien couldn't recall one occasion when Tony had complained.

In fact, Tony seemed glad to put up with all the danger just to be there with him.

Feeling more lonely than ever,
Lucien climbed to the top of the
Smoky Mountain climbing frame.

From up there he could see the
whole camp spread out before him
and for the first time that day,
Lucien felt safe.

Wayne was worried.

He was standing outside the
Three-Eyed Kate toffee-apple stall with
every intention of 'ruining his appetite',
when he realized he wasn't hungry.

In fact, he had a tummy ache.

Wayne didn't get tummy aches
and he was always hungry.

Something's wrong with my 'Fudge Factory',

Gurgle!

he thought to himself and set off to find somewhere cosy to lie down.

Tony had found a way out.

Sitting at the bottom of a bony stair~case, he could see two patches of light way up top.

But Tony was stuck. The bony steps were too steep and as the hours ticked by, he began to think the unthinkable. An escape out of Wayne's southern exit.

Then, without any warning,
Tony's world turned upside down and
he was thrown towards the wall.

Wayne had decided to take a nap
behind the bins and ...

s e i z i n g his chance to escape,
Tony raced towards the light.

His dash for freedom came to an
end in a large echoey chamber.

The only thing in there, apart
from c o b w e b s ...

was a funny grey lump that looked just like a Brussels sprout.

Looking more closely Tony noticed that the lump was covered in m i n u t e writing.

Tony had found Wayne's brain and Wayne's brain was tiny.

Overcome by curiosity, Tony prodded at the bit marked 'eyes open' and that instant the room was f l o o d e d with light.

'This is going to be fun,'

Tony thought to himself and settled down on a lumpy vein to play with his new toy.

Lucien's bum had gone numb and he was about to find a new place to sit, when **disaster struck**.

Lucien Cramp please join your partner at the Square dance barn.

Lucien Cramp to the Square dance barn.

Lucien felt his legs turn to jelly and he quickly climbed down from Smoky Mountain before he fell.

Lucien's first thought was to run away but then he remembered how cruel and unpleasant his mum's beauty treatments could be, and choosing the longest route possible, he set off to the Square dance tent.

Mr Cramp was in the 'Bear pit', enjoying a bout of **manly** back-slapping with his workmates, when he heard his wife calling him from outside.

Fearing that she might let slip another embarrassing pet name, he made an excuse and left.

By the time Mr Cramp caught up with his wife, she was in an hysterical froth and quite unable to speak.

After ten minutes of meaningless babble and arm~waving, Mrs Cramp gave up trying to explain and dragged her husband to the square dance barn instead.

Tony had caused a bit of an accident.

He'd taken Wayne for a little test~
drive and ended up crashing him
into a rubbish bin. Unfortunately
they'd landed upside down and
now Tony couldn't reach
Wayne's movement nodules
to get them out.

Tony had had enough and was about
to make his escape out of Wayne's nostril
when Wayne unexpectedly woke up.

Falling asleep in bins was nothing
new for Wayne but on this occasion
he couldn't remember getting in.

He knew if Mum saw him in here he would be in big trouble, and he got out immediately.

The nap had done wonders for his gut-ache and he sloped off to see how his brother was getting along with the dreaded wendy.

As Lucien had expected, almost all of the dance competitors were girls. The only boys there were little brothers too young or too stupid to know any better.

Lucien was keeping a low profile in the Hog-mask queue when his dance partner arrived.

Lucien almost passed out when she lifted up her Hen mask.

weepy wendy, alias the 'Grand Blubba'.

wendy already had a few small tears in her eyes, when she gave Lucien an ultimatum...

If you do anything, I mean anything rude or nasty you know what will happen don't you!

she sobbed.

Lucien nodded.

He knew exactly what would happen. wendy would cry for a week and Lucien would have to move to **Mars** to escape his mum's make~up bag.

At that moment wayne arrived, covered in crud  and still wearing that same 'I got ya' grin.

Lucien looked away, trying to ignore his irksome sibling.

Tony could see all this through wayne's nose holes and he was hopping mad. Every year wayne pulled a trick like this on Lucien, but this year things would be different...

The Haz Chem junior band struck up to the tune of 'Old MacDonald' and the line of Hogs and Hens were lead out onto the dance floor.

This was the moment Tony had been waiting for.

A chance to give wayne a long cool drink of his own medicine.

Taking hold of wayne's movement nodules, Tony marched him out onto the floor, pushing Lucien to one side as he went.

The idea of Lucien dancing with the Grand Bubba's favourite daughter had made Mr and Mrs Cramp numb with joy.

In fact their eyes were so misty with parental pride, they failed to notice Lucien when he sat down next to them.

The band's version of 'Old MacDonald' came to an untidy end and was hurriedly replaced by a tape of 'Dixieland Melodies'.

The Hogs and Hens began to shuffle about in time to the music and were soon revolving around the floor like some giant insect.

All things considered, Tony was making a rather good job of the 'Two-step Shuffle'.

But Tony knew he wasn't here to practice his dance steps and began manoeuvring Wayne into

the middle of the floor,
in time for the next number.

wayne's  **dirty** outfit had
already raised a few eyebrows, but
it was nothing compared to what
happened   next.

The song had changed to a smoochie ♥
slow dance and this was Tony's cue
to do his stuff.

Taking a firm grip of wayne's
movement nodules, he set about
creating some raunchy new dance steps.

Within seconds the hall was
in **uproar**, with parents rushing
around, pulling their children away
from the dance floor, afraid
for their moral safety.

Mr and Mrs Cramp sank into
their seats, red with shame; and they
weren't the only ones sporting an apple~red
complexion. Tony's hot~blooded dance
routine had come to the attention of

the Grand Bubba himself
and he was burning up
with anger

Bang!

The
Grand Bubba
let off a couple
of rounds from his
Six-Shooter
and the whole show
came to a stop.

Unhand
that
girl!

he yelled.

wayne let loose his grip on wendy and the whole crowd held its breath, waiting for her to turn on the water~works.

It took a few seconds but the effect was spectacular.

waaaaaahhh!!!!

waaaaaahhh!!!!

waaaaaahhh!!!!

By this time the Grand Bubba was eyeball to eyeball with wayne.

What have you got to say for yourself young man!

the Grand Bubba screamed.

Wayne was **speechless** but Tony had one last point to make...

Standing in front of Wayne's nose holes, he prodded the bit of Wayne's brain marked: S n e e z e

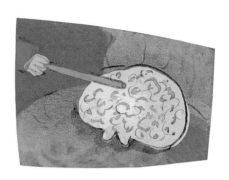

AA~Choooooooo!!!

Hidden in a fine spray
of snot: Tony left wayne's
head at 100 mph and made
a perfect landing on the
Grand Bubba's
ample belly.

The Grand Bubba was Furious.

No one had ever dared to
sneeze on him before and he
was about to call his personal
bodyguard to escort wayne

off the site when he
felt something tugging
on his neck tie.

The Cowboy King looked down
and saw a little green bogyman
waving back at him.

The Grand Bubba collapsed in
a dead faint and Tony made a
dash for the door ...

Gasps of
concern. →

Some weeks later...

The sound of hysterical laughter coming from the front lawn was putting Mr Cramp off his scrubbing rhythm.

He had never guessed that house-work could be so boring, and he was itching to get back to his proper job.

Bleachy whiff

The Grand Bubba had been back at work for weeks, but Mr Cramp was still banned from the factory.

According to the Grand Bubba's intensive care nurse, all members

of the Cramp family
were considered a 'health risk'
and one glimpse of them could
easily trigger a relapse in the
Grand Bubba's condition.

Apparently the Grand Bubba
had been suffering from paranoid
delusions and now made everyone at
the factory wear special nose guards
just in case **bogy monsters**
were hiding in their nostrils.

Mr Cramp decided to go and have his lunch sitting outside the Haz Chem factory gate.

It was a poor substitute for the staff canteen, but at least he could wave to his friends.

As he left the house he noticed Wayne waving to him from the front lawn.

He was helping his mum test a new batch of ever~lasting hair gel, and from where he was standing Mr Cramp thought his son's new hairdo looked very smart indeed.

Wayne was in no position to disagree...

p.t.o.

Mr Cramp **wasn't** the only one who admired wayne's new image. **wendy winkle** had decided that wayne was the **lushest** boy in town.

wayne

Lucien